THE NAME I CALL MYSELF

THE NAME I CALL MYSELF

Text by Hasan Namir

Illustrations by Cathryn John

ARSENAL PULP PRESS
VANCOUVER

ARSENAL PULP PRESS
Suite 202 – 211 East Georgia St.
Vancouver, BC V6A 1Z6
Canada
arsenalpulp.com

The publisher gratefully acknowledges the support of the Canada Council for the Arts and the British Columbia Arts Council for its publishing program, and the Government of Canada, and the Government of British Columbia (through the Book Publishing Tax Credit Program), for its publishing activities.

Arsenal Pulp Press acknowledges the xʷməθkʷəy̓əm (Musqueam), Sḵwx̱wú7mesh (Squamish), and səl̓ilwətaʔɬ (Tsleil-Waututh) Nations, custodians of the traditional, ancestral, and unceded territories where our office is located. We pay respect to their histories, traditions, and continuous living cultures and commit to accountability, respectful relations, and friendship.

This is a work of fiction. Any resemblance of characters to persons either living or deceased is purely coincidental.

Cover illustration by Cathryn John
Back cover and text design by Jazmin Welch
Edited by Shirarose Wilensky

Printed and bound in Korea

Library and Archives Canada Cataloguing in Publication:
Title: The name I call myself / text by Hasan Namir ; illustration by Cathryn John.
Names: Namir, Hasan, 1987– author. | John, Cathryn, 1993– illustrator.
Identifiers: Canadiana (print) 20200200682 | Canadiana (ebook) 20200200755 | ISBN 9781551528090 (softcover) | ISBN 9781551528106 (HTML)
Classification: LCC PS8627.A536 N36 2020 | DDC jC813/.6—dc23

ACKNOWLEDGMENTS

We want to thank everyone at Arsenal Pulp Press for this amazing collaboration. We want to thank our family, friends, and loved ones for their continued love and support. Thank you all so much.

My name is written in front of me.
I try to say it, over and over again.

When I think of the name Edward,
I imagine old kings who snore a lot.

It is the name my parents gave me.
But I call myself something else.

I AM SIX.

I like playing with dolls.
They are awesome superheroes.

My dad cuts my hair so short.
He says, "This is what a boy looks like."

I AM SEVEN.

I idolize my mom.

I especially love the way she wears lipstick.

I have an imaginary friend.

They care about me more than anyone else.

I AM EIGHT.

All my friends are girls.
We have sleepovers and watch princess movies.

My mom says she wishes she had a girl.
Sometimes, I wish I were a girl, too.

I AM NINE.

I want to have long wavy hair.
I want to look like the stars on TV.

My dad says, "You're a boy, so you have to act like one."
Yes, I'm a boy, I'm a boy, I'm a boy.

I AM TEN.

I play a lot of hockey.
But at home, I put on my mom's dresses.

My mom finds out, so I cry.
She says, "Next time, just ask first."

I AM ELEVEN.

I hate my voice so much.
It cracks and breaks, especially when I'm nervous.

I am so embarrassed and scared.
I don't have anyone I can talk to.

I AM TWELVE.

I don't have any real friends.
Everyone calls me Eddie.

My dad catches me kissing Nick Jonas.
It is just a poster, but he yells at me anyway.

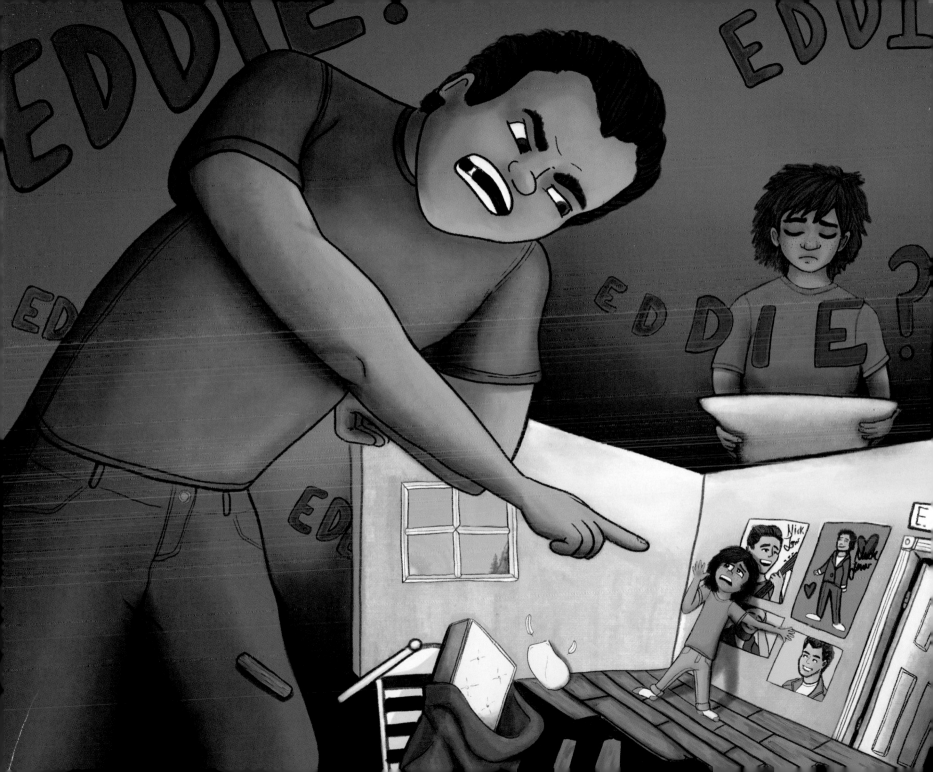

I AM THIRTEEN.

I want to hide the pimples on my face.
My mom lets me borrow her foundation.

I want to disappear from the world.
I don't want people to make fun of me.

I AM FOURTEEN.

I fall in love.

I can't tell my parents about it.

I like doing PE with the boys.

My crush plays hockey with me.

I AM FIFTEEN.

I shave off my body hair.

I pretend I have smooth skin like the girls.

I feel like I don't belong.

Like I'm two people I don't even know anymore.

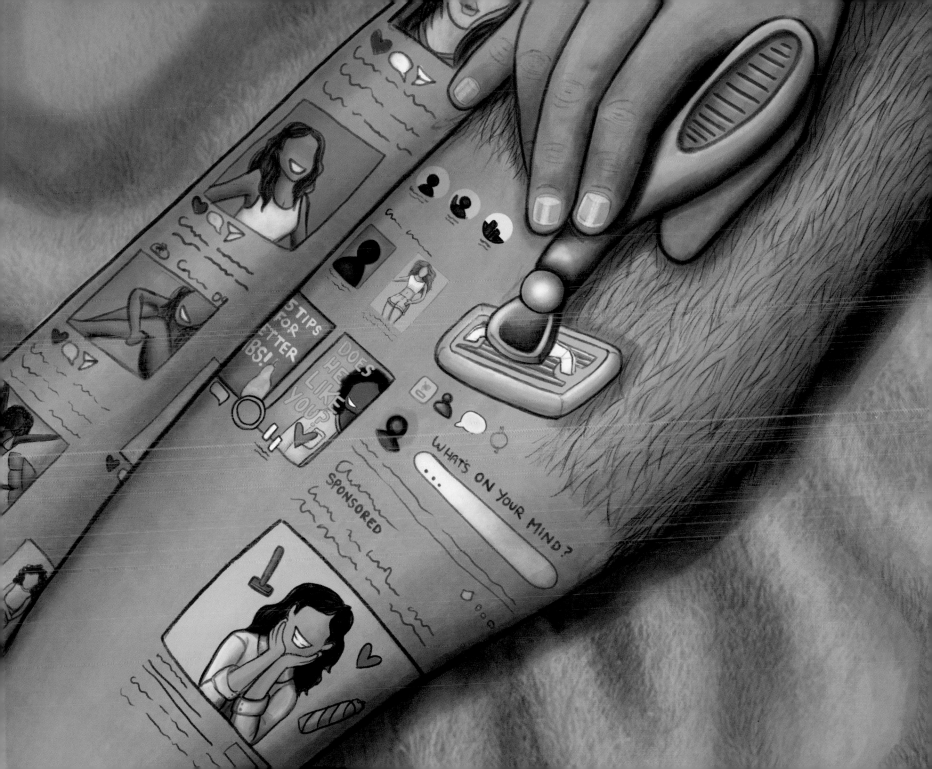

I AM SIXTEEN.

I want to run away.

I want to go somewhere I can be free.

I am so scared to face my dad.

He never listens, not like my mom.

I AM SEVENTEEN.

I don't want to be called Eddie anymore.
Or even Edward.

I feel strong now.
I am ready to face my fears.

I AM EIGHTEEN.

I tell my parents the truth.
I am neither a boy nor a girl.

I don't have to be either of them.
Or I can be both of them at once.

Butterflies are soaring in my stomach.
I can finally be myself.

My name is Ari.
I can be anyone I want to be!

Photo: Alex Ilici

HASAN NAMIR is the author of the Lambda Literary Award–winning novel *God in Pink* and the poetry book *War/Torn* (Book*hug). Born and raised in Iraq, he lives in Vancouver with his partner and their baby.

CATHRYN JOHN is an illustrator and designer with a passion for social equity and the environment. Her practice includes a range of mediums from acrylic painting to woodworking. Cathryn is an international award-winning designer for "The Plant Project," which works to improve people's relationships with plants.